Pawrific Pals

Bath · New York · Cologne · Melbourne · Delhi
Hong Kong · Shenzhen · Singapore · Amsterdam

Welcome to Whisker Haven!

Hearts, hooves, and paws come together in Whisker Haven for friendship and fun! Wave hello to the Palace Pets and their new fluttering friend, Ms. Featherbon.

Splash and Sparkle!

Treasure loves the water so much, she even has her very own pool in the Whisker Haven Pawlace. Petit and Berry have come to visit for a paddle and a splash!

King of the Jungle

The pets love to jump and tumble in Sultan's jungly jungle gym. Pumpkin dances and prances, while Dreamy slips and slides!

Slumber Party

After a busy day at the Pawlace, there's no better place for a rest than Dreamy's dreamy bedroom! While the sleepy kitten settles down for a catnap, Berry settles in for . . . a snack!

Berry

Berry Sweet!

Berry has just finished baking some delicious treats for
her friends. There's enough for everyone—including you!
After all, sharing makes everything sweeter!

Time for Tea

Sultan thinks Ms. Featherbon's atrium is a simply splendificent place for a tea party! It's another magical day in Whisker Haven for the Palace Pets. Best friends fur-ever!

Ariel's kitten, Treasure, is playing in the water when she sees a glowing light coming toward her.

The mysterious light is a magical
hummingbird named Ms. Featherbon.

Ms. Featherbon wants Treasure
to follow her back to Ariel's castle.

Ms. Featherbon shows Treasure a beautiful
Pawlace through a magical door in Ariel's castle.

Treasure leaps through the door and falls into
a tunnel of glittering spirals and twinkling lights.

Ms. Featherbon welcomes Treasure as she tumbles into the Whisker Haven Pawlace.

Find the path that will lead Treasure to Ms. Featherbon.
How many flowers will she collect along the way?
Write your answer in the paw print below.

C

B

A

Treasure loves everything about the ocean!
Can you spot and circle three things below
that Treasure might find under the sea?

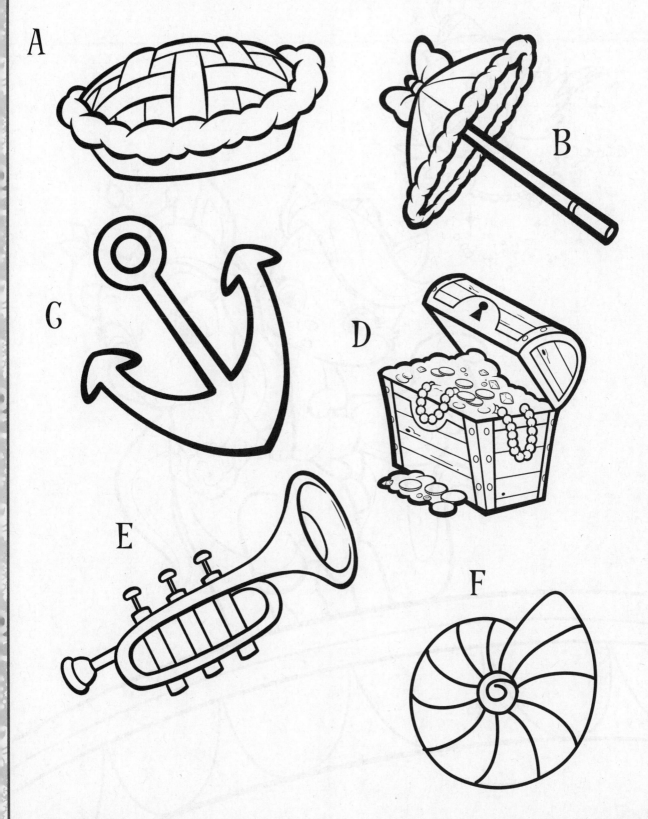

A

B

C

D

E

F

As soon as Treasure arrives, a pony named Petit explains that Pumpkin the puppy is in trouble.

Oh no! Pumpkin's bathtub overflowed
and now the Pawlace has flooded.
Poor Pumpkin is surrounded by water!

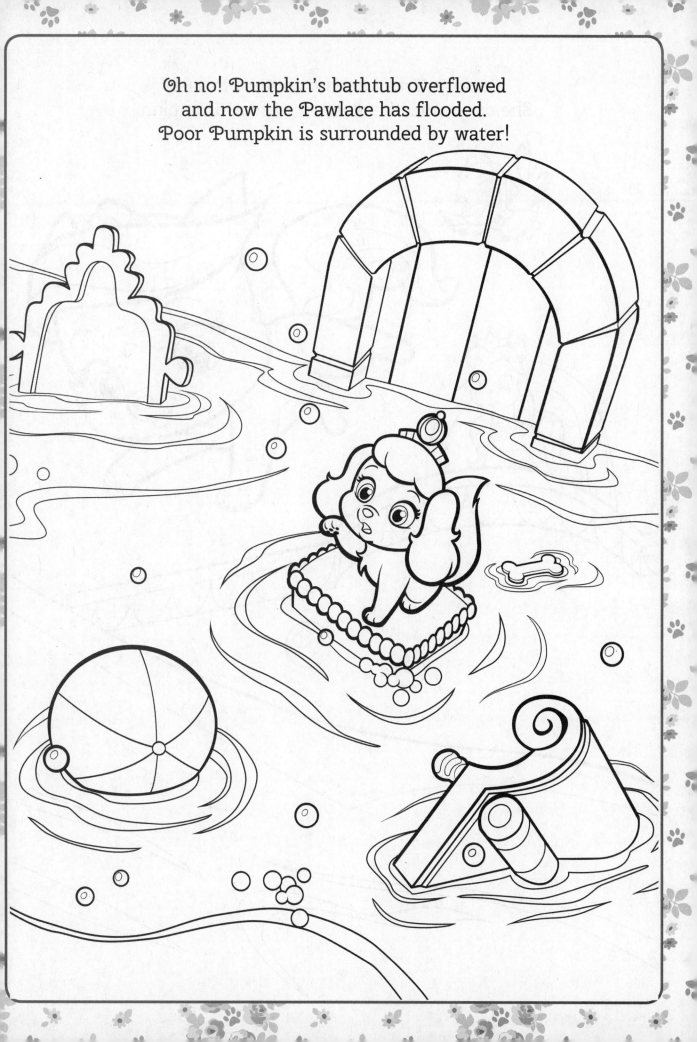

Luckily, Treasure is a great swimmer!
She dives into the water to rescue Pumpkin.

Treasure swims in search of the door to the Pawlace so she can drain the water.

Together, Treasure and Petit pull the door
open and all of the water gushes out!

The royal friends mop and scrub together until
the castle is sparkling clean once again!

Pumpkin and Petit are playing hide-and-seek!
Can you find them hiding somewhere in this scene?

Draw a heart around each pet when
you find them, then color them in!

The Palace Pets are decorating the Great Hall
for a grand celebration called Cake-tillion!

Oops! Sultan runs so fast that
he knocks over Berry's cake!

"But how can we have Cake-tillion without cake?"
Berry wonders. "Don't worry," says Sultan.
"Lily has lots of cakes!"

But Lily has gone missing! The pets gather
around Ms. Featherbon's magical birdbath.
It will tell them where they can find Lily!

The birdbath reveals that Lily is lost in the forest!
Together, the pets begin to search for Lily.

Berry hears a rustling noise nearby.
She uses her ears to guide the pets to Lily.

You're invited to Cake-tillion!
Decorate your very own Whisker Cakes below.
Don't forget to add lots of yummy frosting!

You can use this cupcake as a guide!

Sultan is all dressed up in costume for Cake-tillion!
Find and circle five differences between these two pictures.

Hooray! The Palace Pets have found Lily.
Plus, she has a whole cartload of Whisker Cakes!

Treasure, Lily, and Berry jump into the
cart and enjoy a ride back to the Pawlace.

Sultan pulls the cart as fast as he can to get his friends back to the Pawlace in time for Cake-tillion.

Finally, all the pets have arrived
and there are cakes galore!

"Let the Cake-tillion begin!" calls Ms. Featherbon.
Then all the pets jump into the cakes! *Splat!*

Ms. Featherbon laughs.
"The messier, the better!"

Look at these pictures of Pumpkin, Treasure, and Sultan.
One picture in each row is different from the others.
Can you find the odd one out?

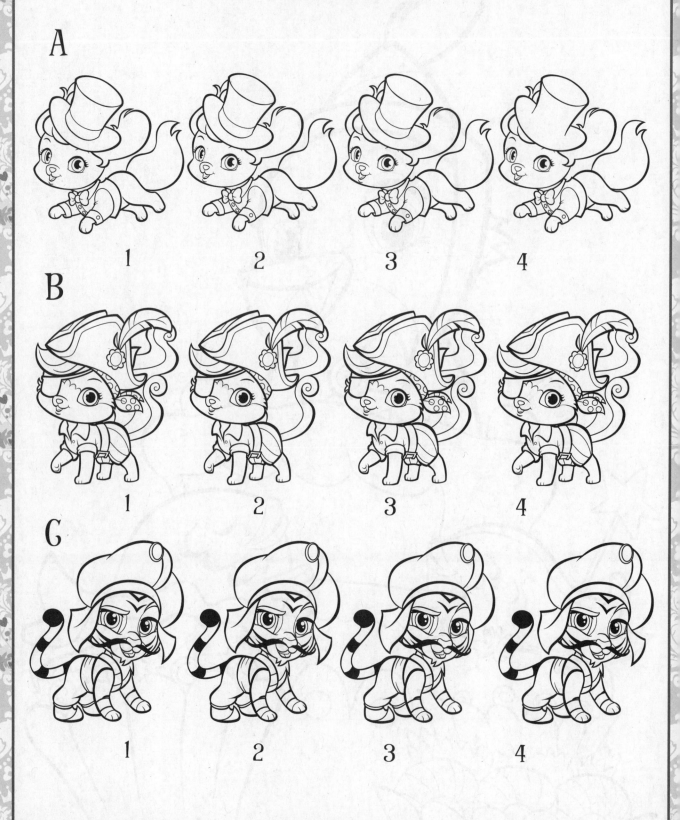

A

1   2   3   4

B

1   2   3   4

C

1   2   3   4